GERMANIA

GERMANIA

Hitler's Twisted Fantasy

ANTHONY GORDON PILLA

ARPress
ILLUMINATING IDEAS
EMPOWERING VOICES

ARPress
45 Dan Road Suite 5
Canton MA 02021

Hotline: 1(888) 821-0229
Fax: 1(508) 545-7580

Ordering Information:

Quantity sales. Special discounts are available on quantity purchases by corporations, associations, and others. For details, contact the publisher at the address above.

Printed in the United States of America.

ISBN-13:   Softcover   979-8-89330-512-8
                eBook   979-8-89330-513-5

Library of Congress Control Number: 2024900511

CONTENTS

PROLOGUE

This is purely a work of fiction. It revises history and cast the United States in the role of mediator rather than warrior. Though this author knows that Adolf Hitler was an evil megalomaniac by skillful negotiating, the lives of six million were saved in this "what if" tale.

DEDICATION

Germania is dedicated to my very special friend - Alfred "MGM AI" Kalbfeld. In his youth AI served his country with honor! In helping to defeat Hitler's Nazi Germany he recieved decorations:

- European Service Medal: one Bronze Star and one Silver Star.

- GO 90 HQ - 9th Air Force - 1945

- Belgium Fourragere: War Department - 1945

Good Life

Portraits
by

Courtney

Christopher

Amerson

FRONT PAGE

The following newspapers were used to tell and illustrate the story:

Germania - Hitler's Twisted Fantasy

Berlin Swastika	Nürnberg Iron Cross
Boston Patriots	Pan American Union
Budapest Twins	Paris Maginot Line
Cairo Pharaoh	Peking Duck
Chimes of London	Pittsburg Hardhats
Dalles Sundial	Plymouth Evening Star
Dresden Pulse	Rome Fascist
Helsinki Vanguard	St. Louis Blues
Istanbul Crescent	Stockholm Dove
Kiev Chicken	Tokyo Rising Sun
Liverpool Current	Vienna Waltz
London Dispatch	Voice of Chicago
Manchester Express	Voice of Munich
Manila Hemp	Washington Digest
Moscow Kremlin	White Cliffs of Dover
New York Eagle	World Jewish Congress

Acknowledgement
Excellent Reference:
RISE AND FALL OF THE THIRD REICH
by William L. Shirer
Simon & Schuster, New York, 1960

SYNOPSIS

Twisted Fantasy

The opening days of the Olympics were making all Germans proud of their Nordic youth winning medals for Germany! Herr Hitler called for parties, dinners and events. After Hitler's state dinner, he retired for the night. During his sleep his mind took him on a journey of Evil vs. Good.

You will see Hitler's version of World War II as his neurotic mind reveals his twisted fantasy.

Berlin ☭ Swastika

BERLIN OLYMPICS - 1936
GERMAN NORDIC VICTORY!

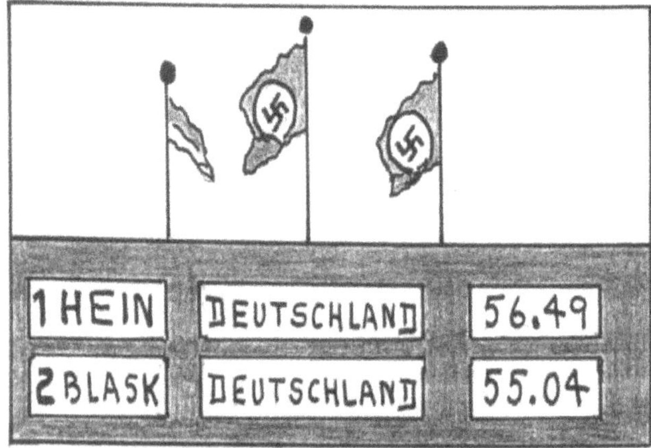

ADOLF HITLER OVERJOYED!

Herr Hitler boasted that our German victories today is just the beginning! We of the Aryan Race will show the world our superiority these next several days. Providence has chosen our German Aryans to be the master race of the world!

The Voice of Munich

ENGLISH EDITION

Warm - Munich, Germany - August 5, 1936

HEIN WINS GOLD
FOR
DEUTSCHLAND!

DRESDEN PULSE

ENGLISH EDITION

WARM - DRESDEN, GERMANY - AUGUST 5, 1936

GERMAN YOUTHS WINNING GOLD AND SILVER MEDALS AT THE BERLIN OLYMPICS

Der Führer has ordered lavish displays of entertainment all over Berlin. High Nazi leaders are planning huge parties for Olympic visitors. Events are scheduled for the duration of the summer games.

Reich Chancellery

August 5, 1936

To Team Officials;
You are cordially invited to send 5 members of your staff to a dinner at the Chancellery on August 7th at 8 P.M. Always in friendship,
Yours,
RSVP   Adolf Hitler

HITLER'S YOUTH
SUPPORT OLYMPIC TEAMS!

August 8, 1936

Herr Hitler:

It has been brought to my attention that German
athletes winning gold medals are invited to your
reviewing box to receive your personal congratulations.
At the same time an African-American winner was
ignored by your leaving the stadium. I.O.C. rules state
that all winners must be honored or none!

By order of the I.O.C.
Chairman Baillet-Latour

Hitler's reaction:
I will not offer personal
congratulations to any athlete!

SYNOPSIS

Lebenstraum

The idea of expanding the "living space" of Germany was a burning obsession of Adolf Hitler. As early as his writing of *Mein Kampf,* he stressed this concept. Now that he is Chancellor of Nazi Germany, he made "Lebenstraum" a major priority of his dream of mastering Europe. Germany must look east! First Austria and Sudetenland and second Slavic Poland and Russia!

VIENNA WALTZ

ENGLISH EDITION

COOL	VIENNA, AUSTRIA	APRIL 13, 1938

GERMAN ANNEXATION OF AUSTRIA!

In a February 20, 1938, speech, Adolf Hitler promised protection to ten million Germans living outside the Reich! Germany issued an ultimatum to the Austrian Chancellor Schuschunigg to resign. Unable to resist he resigned. The new Austrian Chancellor Seyss-Inquart appealed to Hitler to send troops to restore order. On March 12th German troops invaded our country! No resistance was offered. Chancellor Seyss-Inquart proclaimed our union with Germany. On April 12th a plebiscite was held which resulted in a 99.5% vote in favor of union with Deutschland!

Berlin 卐 Swastika

<table>
<tr><td>Fair</td><td>Berlin · Germany</td><td>September 23, 1938</td></tr>
</table>

GERMAN-CZECH CRISIS

Herr Hitler's Nürnberg speech on September 12th demanded Prague leaders grant right of "self-determination" to Germans living in the Sudetenland region of Czechoslovakia.

British Prime Minister Neville Chamberlain proposed a personal conference with the Führer.

Berchtesgarden September 15th Meeting: Herr Hitler told Chamberlain that he wanted to annex Sudetenland to Germany. Hitler was ready to risk a war to attain his goal.

Godesberg September 22nd Meeting: Hitler demanded a plebiscite be held in the Sudetenland. Chamberlain regarded Hitler's demand as unacceptable and as an unwarranted extension of his original demands.

The Chimes of London

Fair	London, England	October, 1 1938

HIGHLIGHTS OF MUNICH PACT

September 28

Herr Hitler invited European leaders to a conference in Munich, Germany, to resolve the crisis in Czechoslovakia.

September 29

Principal leaders at the conference

Adolf Hitler - Germany

Benito Mussolini - Italy

Edouard Daladier - France

Neville Chamberlain - Britain

Topic:

Sudetenland: Czech or Reich?

October 1

Agreement:

1. Hitler secured all that he demanded.
2. Czech evacuation of all the Sudetenland to take place between October 1-10, 1938.
3. France and Britain to guarantee new frontiers of Czechoslovakia.
4. Prague government impelled to acquiesce to the settlement.

Chamberlain at No. 10 Downing St. "Peace in Our Time"

Berlin 卐 Swastika

| Clear | Berlin - Germany | March 21, 1939 |

GERMANY MUST LOOK EASTWARD

HITLER'S "LEBENSTRAUM" POLICY!

1938 - ANNEXATION OF AUSTRIA

1939 - ANNEXATION OF SUDETENLAND (1)

1940 - ANNIHILATION OF CZECHOSLOVAKIA (2)

GERMAN - SOVIET
NONAGGRESSION TREATY

During the week of August 15-21, intense diplomatic communications and visits between leaders of Berlin and Moscow produced a pact between our two countries which was signed on August 21, 1939.

Treaty provisions:

1. Baltic states to join the U.S.S.R.
2. Bessarabia to be returned to Russia (given to Rumania in 1919 treaty)
3. German diplomacy will be used to influence an improvement in Russo-Japanese relations.
4. Poland will be partitioned between Germany and the Union of Soviet Socialist Republics.

Warm | Paris, France | September 2, 1939

GERMANY + RUSSIA INVADE POLAND!

September 1, 1939

BREAKING NEWS
FRANCE AND BRITAIN DECLARE WAR ON GERMANY!
WORLD WAR II BEGINS !

Cloudy — Tokyo, Japan — September 28, 1940

3-POWERS PACT

Herr Hitler announced that the Italian *Duce* Benito Mussolini and our prince Fumumaro Konoye - Prime Minister of Japan, meeting in Berlin, concluded a three-powers pact pledging total aid to all members for a period of ten years! The goal of the pact is to promote the prosperity of all the people!

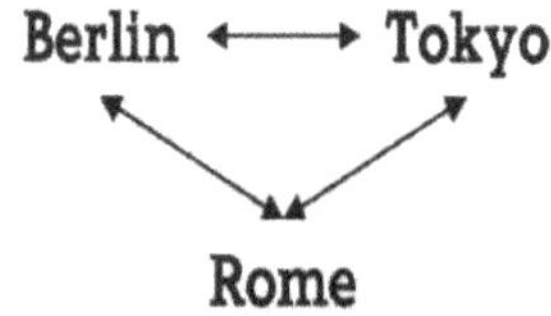

AXIS POWERS

The three contracting powers further promised mutual assistance in the event any one became involved in a war with a power not then a belligerent.

SITZKRIEG: 1939 - 1940
"Sit-Down War" - Nazis
"Phony War" - Brits

After the disposal of Poland by the Nazis and Soviets, both sides called for peace in Europe. After France and Britain declared war - but never attacked Germany, public opinion grew to call this a "Queer kind of war." French and Germans faced each other, but no action! U-boats did sink British ships, but Hitler ordered his military to move slowly. The extreme cold '39 - '40 winter shut-down military preparations. Only the short-lived Soviet-Finnish war disturbed the peace of Europe. Hitler stated that he had no war aims against France and Britain, and called for an all European peace conference. Der Führer secretly issued directive No. 6 "Prepare for War." P.M. Chamberlain called on Hitler to give proof, not words, of peace. We all know, Hitler's military occupied Denmark and Norway - Low Countries are next? Thus - **ENDS THE SITZKRIEG!**

SYNOPSIS

Oktoberfest Blitzkrieg...

Using the excuse that the Reich must protect Denmark and Norway from an Anglo-French invasion, Hitler ordered a sudden occupation. Britain and France made an attempt to repulse the Blitzkrieg, but failed! Hitler then ordered: The Victory of the West The Low Countries fell followed by France. The combined Anglo-French military force had to surrender at Dunkirk. However, as you shall see, a miracle will change the course of history!

OKTOBERFEST BLITZKRIEG ENDS SITZKRIEG...

Columns of Wehrmacht troops crossed into Denmark and occupied without resistance!

German naval and airborne Divisions descended on Norway

Anglo-French Expeditionary forces landed in Southern Norway	German forces compelled Anglo-French forces to withdraw

GLORIOUS NEWS . . .

GERMAN TROOP SUPERIORITY BROKE THE BACK OF THE NORWEGIAN RESISTANCE MOVEMENT

DENMARK AND NORWAY ARE NOW PART OF GERMANY

Nürnberg Iron Cross

ENGLISH EDITION

Rain   Nürnberg, Germany   October 6, 1940

GERMANY INVADES DENMARK AND NORWAY

ARMED FORCES OF THE THIRD REICH MARCHED THROUGH THE STREETS OF COPENHAGEN TOWARDS THE DANISH ROYAL PALACE

STUNNED DANISH CITIZENS STOOD BY AND WATCHED OUR TROOPS ENTER THEIR CITY!

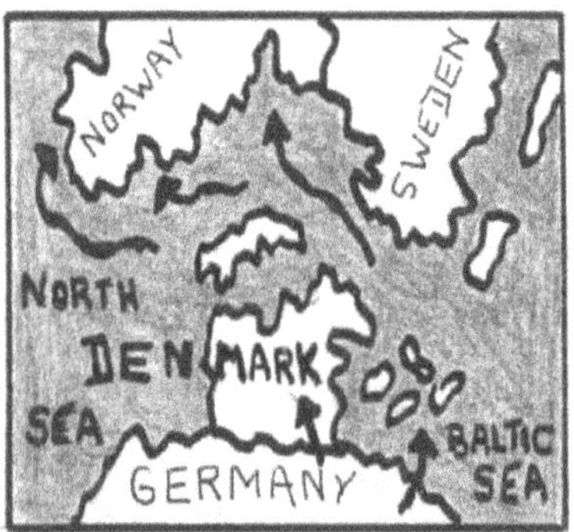

War Ministry announcement:
Telephone exchanges and radio stations were
seized by the Quisling Government. German air
borne forces control Norway's ports!

The Chimes of London

Fair   London, England   October, 7 1940

BRITISH NAVAL UNITS ATTACKED GERMAN SHIPS IN NARVICK, NORWAY

PORT OF NARVICK RE-CAPTURED!

Anglo-French expeditionary forces were compelled to withdraw from Norway due to reinforced German troops

German Reich Commissar for Norway – Joseph Terboven appointed Vidkun Quisling "Minister-President" of occupied Norway. Quisling abolished Norwegian constitution and appointed himself

DICTATOR OF NORWAY

QUISLING NOW MEANS TRAITOR!

PARIS MAGINOT LINE

ENGLISH EDITION

Rain	Paris, France	October 29, 1940

GERMAN FORCES LAUNCH BLITZKRIEG INVASION OF NETHERLANDS, BELGIUM AND LUXEMBURG!

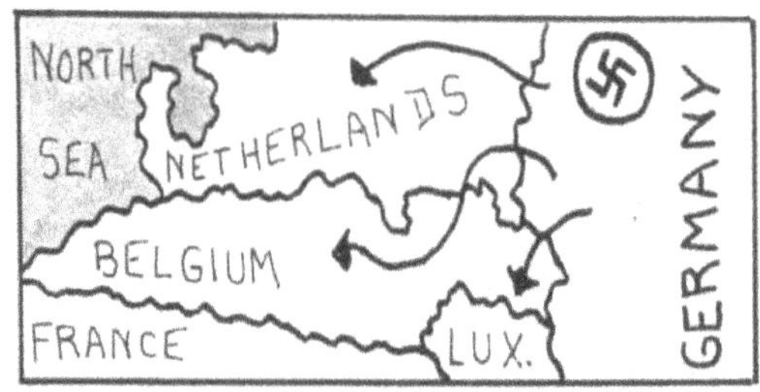

FRENCH AND BRITISH FORCES ASSIST BELGIUM'S RESISTANCE.

ROTTERDAM SURRENDERS AFTER EXTERMINATING AIR ATTACKS.

DUTCH ARMY CAPITULATED!

> WILL THE GREAT MAGINOT LINE PROTECT FRANCE?

VOICE OF CHICAGO

5¢   Windy   Chicago, Illinois   November 3, 1940

PRESIDENTIAL CAMPAIGN OF 1940
CONVENTION HIGHLIGHTS

Republican Convention meet in Philadelphia on June 28. Wendell L Willkie won the nomination for President. In a "back room" deal he picked the popular American Hero - Charles A. Lindbergh to be his vice-president. Lindbergh is to be given "wide powers" in foreign affairs.

On July 18, the Democrats, here in Chicago, nominated for a third term, Franklin D. Roosevelt. FDR pledged to keep America out of foreign wars!

CAMPAIGN TRAIL

Willkie 'n Lindy - two terms good enough for Washington, good enough for FDR - two terms deserve another!

NATIONAL POLL TRACKING		
DATE	FDR	WLW
August	67.3	32.7
September	56.6	43.4
October	53.5	46.5
November	50.1	49.9

June 26, 1940

MEMORANDUM OF UNDERSTANDING
BETWEEN
WENDELL L. WILLKIE and CHARLES A. LINDBERGH

I, Charles A. Lindbergh, agree to support

Wendell Willkie for the nomination as

president at the Republican Convention in

Philadelphia on June 28, 1940.

I, Wendell L. Willkie, shall select Charles

A. Lindbergh to be my vice presidential

running mate if nominated by our party.

I further agree to give my vice president

broad powers in conducting foreign affairs.

5 c   Warm   St. Louis, Missouri   November 6, 1940

WENDELL WILLKIE DEFEATS FDR!

REPUBLICANS CAPTURE CONTROL OF CONGRESS

POPULAR VOTE	ELECTORAL VOTE
WLW: 24,371,861	WLW: 283
FDR: 23,563,952	FDR: 252

WILLKIE WON : NORTH AND SOUTH
ROOSEVELT WON : SOLID SOUTH

EDITORIAL

The American voters wanted
a new team - "grass roots"
Willkie and **Lucky Lindy**.
Men with NEW VISIONS!

PARIS MAGINOT LINE

ENGLISH EDITION

| Fair | Paris, France | November 7, 1940 |

PARIS DECLARED AN "OPEN CITY"

OKTOBERFEST BLITZKRIEG
★ THE B + B WAR ★

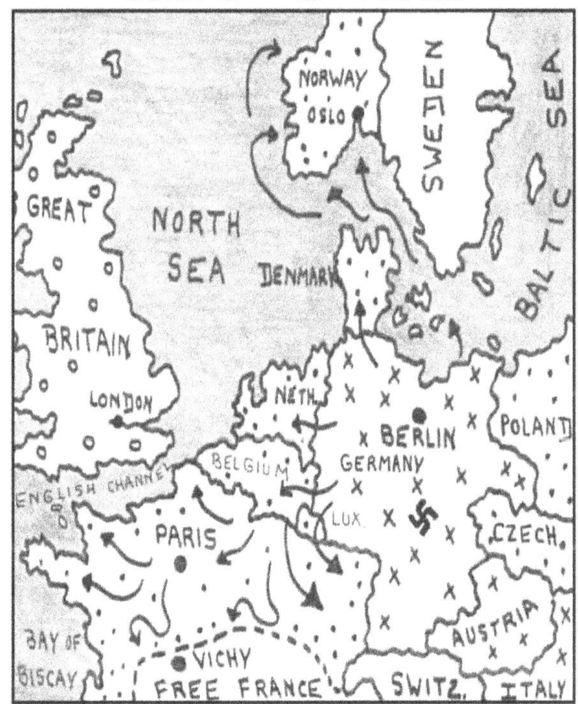

VICTORY IN THE WEST !

Nürnberg Iron Cross

ENGLISH EDITION

Cold	Nürnberg, Germany	November 30, 1940

HIGHLIGHTS OF THE WAR IN THE WEST

TIMELINE OF EVENTS

Nov. 3 - German forces invade France

Nov. 4 - Fall of Brussels

Nov. 5 - Italy declares war on France

Nov. 7 - Paris declared an "Open City"

Nov. 10 - German forces capture Paris

Nov. 15 - B.E.F. and French troops at Dunkirk

Nov. 22 - Marshal Henri Petain asked Hitler for an armistice

Nov. 23 - Der Führer agreed to an armistice

Nov. 27 - King Leopold III ordered Belgium forces to capitulate

Nov. 28 - The armistice between France and Germany was signed at Compeign, France. France agreed to disarm and surrender 3/5 of her land

Nov. 29 - A French government was created at Vichy. Marshal Petain and Pierre Laval became puppet rulers.

New York Eagle

5 ¢   Fair   New York, New York   December 3, 1940

SURRENDER AT DUNKIRK!

With their backs to the English Channel, 250,000 British and 120,000 French troops were trapped on a narrow beach called: Dunkirk. While they fought defiantly, hoping for a miracle, General Heinz Guderian's 1st and 2nd panzers proved to be too powerful, which resulted in a total loss to superior German forces.

The Miracle of Dunkirk?

In recent presidential election, the popular peace-advocate, Charles A. Lindbergh, was elected vice president.

Lindbergh called on Herr Hitler and Britain to negotiate an end to this war!

New York Eagle

5 ¢   Fair   New York, New York   December 3, 1940

Lindbergh's Miracle!

In a fury of trans-Atlantic cables sent on Dec. 3rd to Hitler, the Duke of Windsor, Mussolini, Pope Pious XII and the King of Sweden, the vice president-elect was able to arrange a summit of Anglo-German diplomats to be held in Stockholm on Dec. 6 and 7, 1940. The King of Sweden to host this conference at the Royal Palace. Since Charles A. Lindbergh has no powers until his inauguration on January 20, 1941, his attendance will be only as an observer.

Chancellor Hitler accepted the Lindbergh idea only if Britain sends the former King Edward VIII, now Duke of Windsor, and former Prime Minister Neville Chamberlain to Stockholm. Prime Minister Winston Churchill demanded that Parliament reject this idea. To a shocked Churchill, Parliament under intense pressure to return the B.E.F., voted to attend!

English Edition

| Cold | Stockholm, Sweden | December 7, 1940 |

TREATY OF STOCKHOLM

**After two days of intense talks, Germany and
Britain agreed on peace terms.
Our King announced - the signing of the treaty will
take place tonight at 8PM in the State Room of the
Royal Palace**

TERMS OF AGREEMENT

GERMANY

1. Return B.E.F. to Britain
2. End naval blockade
3. Freedom of the Seas
4. French troops to Vichy
5. Free World Trade
6. Exodus policy for all
   European Jews to homeland
   in Palestine: Adhere to
   Balfour declaration of 1917.

GREAT BRITAIN

1. Policy of Neutrality
2. Free Neutral Ireland, India,
   Australia, Canada, New
   Zealand and South Africa
3. Gibraltar to Spain
4. Falklands to Argentina
5. Malta to Italy
6. Cyprus to Turkey
7. Channel Island to Germany
8. Hong-Kong and Singapore to
   Japan

CONCLUDING REMARKS:

Chancellor Hitler:

I wish to express my admiration
of the British Empire, of the ne-
cessity for its existence and of the
civilization that Britain had
brought into the world. All I want
from Britain is that she should
acknowledge Germany's position
on the continent of Europe

Duke of Windsor:

I wish to pay special tribute to
the Führer's desire for peace,
which is in complete agreement
with my point of view. I am firmly
convinced that if I had been king,
it would never have come to war.

THE WHITE HOUSE
WASHINGTON, D.C.

Date: December 8, 1940
To: Vice President Lindbergh
From: President Willkie
Subject: Foreign Affairs

I wish to express my utmost pleasure with your

role in the Stockholm affair. Your involvement as a

mediator helped to pull off the Dunkirk Miracle! I am

therefore expanding the scope of your role to include

representing me at all summits and conferences.

All I require you to do is to keep me informed on all

aspects of your involvement. My main concern is for

you to keep America out of wars, and develop a

working relationship with the Axis Powers.

Washington Digest

Windy   Washington, D.C.   December 8, 1940   5¢

BREAKING NEWS . . .
GREAT BRITAIN SURRENDERS COLONIES TO AXIS POWERS!

Terms of the
ANGLO - GERMAN
STOCKHOLM
PEACE TREATY

LIVERPOOL CURRENT

Rain | Liverpool, England | December 8, 1940

LONDON IN "GRAVE TURMOIL" OVER TREATY!

THOUSANDS OF ANGRY CITIZENS STORMED HYDE PARK TO VENT THEIR FRUSTRATIONS

Manchester Express

| Cool | Manchester, England | December 9, 1940 |

PUBLIC OUTCRY ALL OVER THE UNITED KINGDOM!

CONFLICTS RAGING OVER THE ANGLO-NAZI PEACE TREATY

"SIT-INS" REPORTED AT BUCKINGHAM PALACE AND TRAFALGAR SQUARE. MASS DEMONSTRATIONS AT HYDE PARK!

PARLIAMENT UNDER PRESSURE:
TELEGRAMS - LETTERS - PETITIONS
AND TELEPHONE MESSAGES ARE
POURING INTO PARLIAMENT BY
THE THOUSANDS!
REPORTS INDICATE THAT:
55% ARE PRO-TREATY
45% ARE CON-TREATY
MOST EDITORIALS ARE ANTI TREATY
MOTHERS-AGAINST-THE-WAR: GROWING!

Plymouth Evening Star

Fair   Plymouth, England   December 9, 1940

VERBAL WAR RAGES ON
IN HOUSES OF PARLIAMENT
OVER STOCKHOLM PEACE TREATY!

M.P.'s SHOUTING:

SELL OUT TO THE NAZIS – BRITANNIA STILL
RULES THE WAVES – GIVE PEACE A CHANCE –
ENGLAND FIRST – SAVE OUR B.E.F. BOYS –
NEW DARK AGE! – NO LONGER OUR FINEST
HOUR – NEUTRALITY GOOD FOR AMERICA:
GOOD ENOUGH FOR BRITAIN – BRING THE
250,000 TROOPS HOME!

London Dispatch

Rain   London, England   December 10, 1940

BY A MARGIN OF TWENTY VOTES PARLIAMENT APPROVES TREATY!

STUNNED, WINSTON CHURCHILL STORMED OUT OF THE HOUSE OF COMMONS AND RETURNED TO THE P.M.'S RESIDENCE AT 10 DOWNING ST.!

CHURCHILL IMMEDIATELY INFORMED KING GEORGE VI THAT HE WAS GOING TO "STEP DOWN" AS PRIME MINISTER

London Dispatch

Fog   London, England   December 11, 1940

CHURCHILL RESIGNS!

In a radio address to the nation, Winston Churchill stated that the sun has now set on the British Empire!

"I will never agree to the surrender of our heritage to the likes of Adolf Hitler. Therefore, I will retire from public service and return to private life at Chartwell, to meditate by the pond and my life long joy - painting!"

London Dispatch

| Fog | London, England | December 11, 1940 |

CHAMBERLAIN RETURNS AS PRIME MINISTER

At the urgent request of the Duke of Windsor, and the strong demand of the pacifist mood of Parliament, King George VI called on Neville Chamberlain to form a new government and direct the United Kingdom on a course of neutrality in world affairs. Thus, Britain joined the United States on an Anglo-American path of neutrality. In Parliament, Chamberlain's doves beat Churchill's hawks and approved Chamberlain as the new Prime Minister of Great Britain!

God Save the King

London Dispatch

Fair	London, England	December 14, 1940

Exclusive dispatch . . .

Reich Chancellery

December 13, 1940

Chamberlain:

On Behalf of the German people, who have much in common with the people of England, I wish you success as Prime Minister.

To show that I am looking for a new Anglo-American relationship, I have issued the following directives:

1. U-Boat blockade of Britain will cease as of 0600 GMT on December 14.
2. All B.E.F. troops will be released at 0800 GMT on December 14. British navy will have safe passage to pick up all 250,000 troops.
3. All issues agreed at Stockholm will be mutually carried out!

Yours,
Adolf Hitler

Washington Digest

Cold   Washington, D.C.   January 16, 1941   5¢

FDR'S FAREWELL FIRESIDE CHAT TO THE AMERICAN PEOPLE

The foundation of our republic is based on the bedrock principles of freedom and democracy. Last November the will of the American people was expressed in a desire to have a new captain of our ship of state! For eight years you have entrusted me to sail our ship through rough waters. I have navigated her through the treacherous waters of the Great Depression, stating that the only thing we have to fear is fear itself! While the currents are calmer now, I fear that the winds are gathering ominous clouds on the horizon, which may place our ship in harm's way! On January 20, 1941, a new captain must guide us through the angry sea. I salute him, and may Providence give him the skills to stir our course safely. Goodbye, and may God bless America!

Radio address: January 15th

Boston Patriots 5¢

Snow   Boston, Massachusetts   January 21, 1941

WILLKIE'S INAUGURAL ADDRESS

1. He enunciated a corollary to the Monroe Doctrine - American continents are hence forth neutral in all wars of European or Asiatic powers.
2. He will call upon Hitler to honor his pledge to adhere to the Balfour Declaration which calls for a homeland for Jews.
3. He will call on all neutral nations to help Jews to exodus to Palestine.
4. He will ask Congress to admit 100,000 Jews to America under the exodus provisions of the Stockholm Treaty.
5. He intends to make America the arsenal of humanitarian protection for all oppressed war victims.
6. He will call for a summit of Axis powers and key neutral countries to create a human rights charter for all people of occupied lands.
7. He assured the American people that our military posture will be strong, modernized and capable to meet all challenges to our national defense!

DRESDEN PULSE

ENGLISH EDITION

COLD — DRESDEN, GERMANY — MARCH 2, 1941

THREE POWERS PACT EXPANDS TO SIX AXIS POWERS PACT

The Reich Chancellery announced
the expansion of the Three Axis
Powers Pact: Berlin-Rome-Tokyo!

Hungary : November 20, 1940
Rumania : November 23, 1940
Bulgaria : March 1, 1941

Chancellor Adolf Hitler:
All Germans should be pleased
to see our world-wide support

HEIL HITLER

PITTSBURG HARDHATS

5¢

Warm   Pittsburg, Pennsylvania   May 21, 1941

GERMAN-AMERICAN SUMMIT?

Rumors are running wild in D.C. that Adolf Hitler would like to meet with the vice president who was awarded the Service Cross of the German Eagle - Charles A. Lindbergh! Numerous trans-Atlantic cables have been exchanged. It has been reported that the vice president agreed to meet with the Reich Chancellor. Secretary of State Thomas E. Dewey hinted that a summit in the Azores might take place in mid-June.

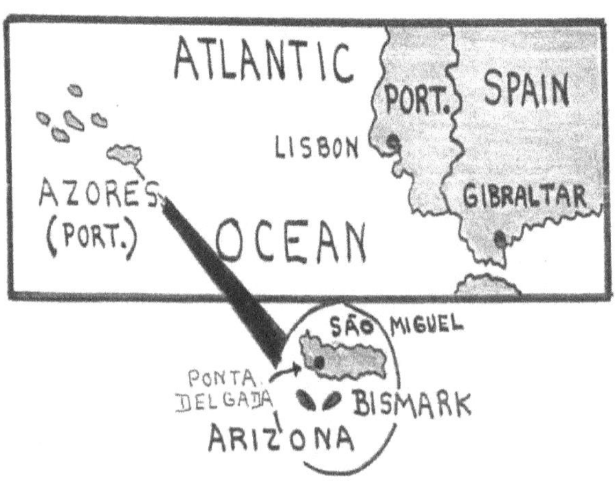

Dalles ☀ Sundial

| Hot | Dalles, Texas | June 7, 1941 | 5¢ |

ATLANTIC CHARTER

VICE PRESIDENT LINDBERGH AND CHANCELLOR HITLER HELD TALKS ON JUNE 5 AND 6 NEAR THE AZORES ON BATTLESHIPS: ARIZONA AND BISMARCK

AGREEMENTS:

1. Freedom of the sea for all Axis and neutral nations.
2. Humane treatment and basic rights for all occupied people.
3. Development of an exodus plan for European Jews to Palestine. For now, Jews are restricted to detention centers under supervision of the International Red Cross.
4. Neutral powers are to respect government affairs of Axis nations.
5. Axis powers are to give full assurance to all neutrals: non-interference in all domestic and foreign affairs.
6. Both leaders urged the formation of an international organization to maintain world peace and security.

SYNOPSIS

Operation Barbarossa

With France defeated and occupied, and Britain reduced to the status of a neutral nation, the only country blocking Hitler from becoming the master of Europe was Russia. In Hitler's mind, Russia must be liquidated, and sooner the better! Barbarossa was the military code given for the invasion. To conquer the vast Russian lands, Germany needed to form a coalition of Axis powers. Invasion was launched at 0600 Hrs. on September 14, 1941.

MOSCOW KREMLIN

English Edition

Warm	Moscow, U.S.S.R.	September 15, 1941

GERMAN INVASION

AXIS POWERS LAUNCH A 2,000 MILE FRONT FROM
THE WHITE SEA TO THE BLACK SEA WITH A MILITARY
FORCE OF 121 DIVISIONS AND 3,000 PLANES.
665,000 PRISONERS TAKEN!

STALIN CALL FOR GENERAL MOBILIZATION

English · Helsinki, Finland · September 18, 1941

FINLAND

DECLARES WAR ON THE

SOVIET UNION!

FINNISH TROOPS JOINS - OPERATION BARBAROSSA AND INVADES RUSSIA GOAL IS TO CAPTURE LENINGRAD!

| English | Kiev, Ukraine | September 19, 1941 |

UKRAINE JOINS AXIS POWERS

SECRET AGREEMENT:

GERMAN AND UKRAINIAN DIPLOMATS AND MILITARY LEADERS HELD 3 DAYS OF SECRET TALKS IN A HIDDEN RESORT IN THE CARPATHIAN MOUNTAINS LAST AUGUST!

ITEMS OF AGREEMENT:

1. On the 3rd day of Operation Barbarossa, Ukrainian National Guard and State Police were to control all forms of communications, rail and transportation centers. They were to join forces with Axis military units as they capture all Soviet held areas of the Ukraine.
2. After the complete destruction of the Soviet Communist regime, the Ukraine was to gain all Russian land west of the Urals and south of Leningrad.

DEATH TO STALIN

HELSINKI VANGUARD

English   Helsinki, Finland   October 1, 1941

LENINGRAD - "OPEN CITY" SOVIETS SURRENDER!

After ten days of military siege, Soviet General Nikita Chuikov notified Finnish Field Headquarters that he would surrender Leningrad and declare it to be an "open city" as of 1500 Hrs. on 30 September, 1941.

HELSINKI RENAMED THE CITY: ST. PETERSBURG !

English   Kiev, Ukraine   October 4, 1941

FALL OF STALINGRAD

COALITION OF AXIS FORCES: UKRAINE • GERMANY • RUMANIA • ITALY AND BULGARIA FORCED 355,000 SOVIET TROOPS TO **SURRENDER!**

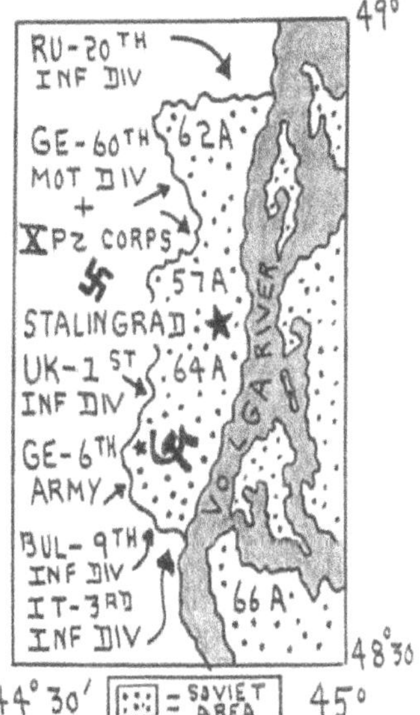

COLLAPSE OF THE U.S.S.R IS JUST WEEKS AWAY!

TURKEY ATTACKS SOVIET TROOPS IN GEORGIA— ARMENIA AND AZERBAIJAN

OPERATION BARBAROSSA - AXIS INVASION OF THE U.S.S.R. CALLS ON TURKISH FORCES TO CAPTURE THE RICH OIL FIELDS OF BAKU ON THE CASPIAN SEA!

Berlin Swastika

Warm   Berlin - Germany   October 7, 1941

ON TO MOSCOW!

HERR HITLER'S ORDER:
"ENCIRCLE THEM—BEAT THEM—DESTROY THEM"

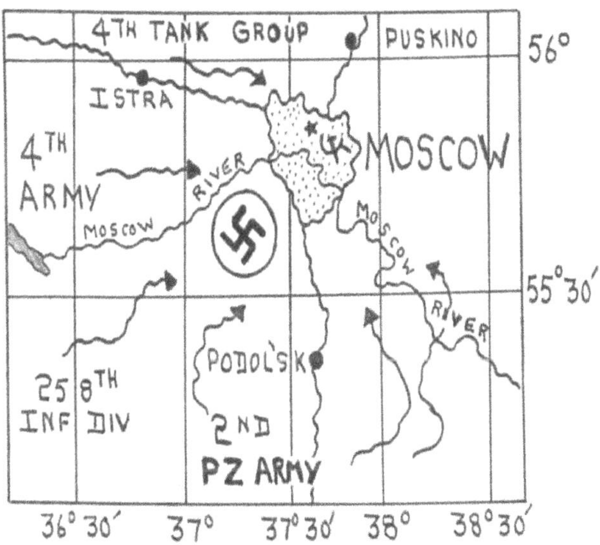

TO GERMAN HIGH COMMAND:
KICK IN THE DOOR AND THE WHOLE
ROTTEN STRUCTURE WILL COME
CRASHING DOWN .

Adolf Hitler

MOSCOW KREMLIN

English Edition

Fair   Moscow, U.S.S.R.   October 9, 1941

GOERING'S LUFTWAFFE BOMBING MOSCOW!

DAY 1

LONG LIVE MOTHER RUSSIA

MOSCOW KREMLIN

English Edition

| Fair | Moscow, U.S.S.R. | October 10, 1941 |

MOSCOW ON FIRE!

DAY 2

MOSCOW KREMLIN

English Edition

RASPUTITIZA?

It was reported to the Moscow Kremlin that Chairman Joseph Stalin was overheard shouting at his weather advisers - Where is Rasputitiza? And Mother Russia's favorite general - Winter?

For our readers, Chairman Stalin was referring to the annual October rains which is the period of mud! This would slow down Hitler's <u>Operation Typhoon</u> to a slow crawl. This precious time would allow General Winter to come down on the Nazi war machine and protect Russia with a severe winter! Remember Napoleon's *Conquest of Moscow*? The winter of 1812 proved to be a disaster for the retreating French grand army!

Berlin ☒ Swastika — English Edition

Rain   Berlin · Germany   October 24, 1941

MOSCOW CAPTURED!
STALIN FLEES CITY
SOVIET MARSHAL WANTS AN ARMISTICE

SMOLENSK SURRENDER:

Surrender of the Soviet Army by Marshal Zingkof, Soviet Supreme Commander, was signed at 1350 hrs. on 23 October, 1941. General Alfred Jodl, Wehrmacht Chief of Staff, signed for Germany and all other Axis powers.

TERMS OF SURRENDER:

1. Armistice line along the Ural Mountains to be established on 29 October, 1941.
2. All Soviet military personnel are to be disarmed and move to the free Slavic land, as well as civilians.
3. All Soviet land, except Leningrad, are to become part of Ukraine.

HITLER'S SPEECH TO THE WORLD
LAST NIGHT - HERR HITLER TOLD THE WORLD THAT PEACE IN EUROPE IS AT LAST UPON US!

English   Kiev, Ukraine   October 31, 1941

OPERATION BARBAROSSA—
DEFEATS THE SOVIET UNION!

COALITION OF AXIS FORCES:
(1)ITALY (2) BULGARIA (3) RUMANIA
(4) GERMANY (5) UKRAINE (6) FINLAND (7)
TURKEY

DISSARMED RUSSIANS ALLOWED TO LIVE IN F.S.L
EAST OF THE AGREED ARMISTICE LINE

AXIS POWERS
Public Information Office
PRESS RELEASE
January 31, 1942

<u>YALTA ACCORDS</u>
January 12 - 30, 1942

The principal leaders of the victorious Axis powers over the Communist Soviet Union met in Yalta, Crimea to confer on plans for re-establishing peace and order in the defeated U.S.S.R.

DECISIONS REACHED:

1. Council of foreign ministers, representing: Germany, Italy, Finland, Hungary, Rumania, Bulgaria, Ukraine and Turkey will be created to continue the task of drafting peace settlements.

(page one of two)

2. Conditions of former Soviet union:

A) Disarm and demilitarize

B) Dissolve the communist Party

C) Trial of War Criminals

D) Restore local civil authorities

E) Military security

F) Russians have a choice: live in Ukraine or relocate to the F.S.L.

3. To the victors belong the spoils

A) Finland to receive Leningrad and the Baltic States

B) Ukraine to gain the former Russia, S.S.R. to the Urals

C) Germany to receive the Polish lands occupied by the Soviet Union in the 1939 invasion of Poland

D) Germany, Hungary, Rumania, Bulgaria and Turkey to receive annually 15%, and Ukraine 25% of Baku oil production

(page two of two)

HITLER'S DIRECTIVE: MOSCOW - NO MORE!

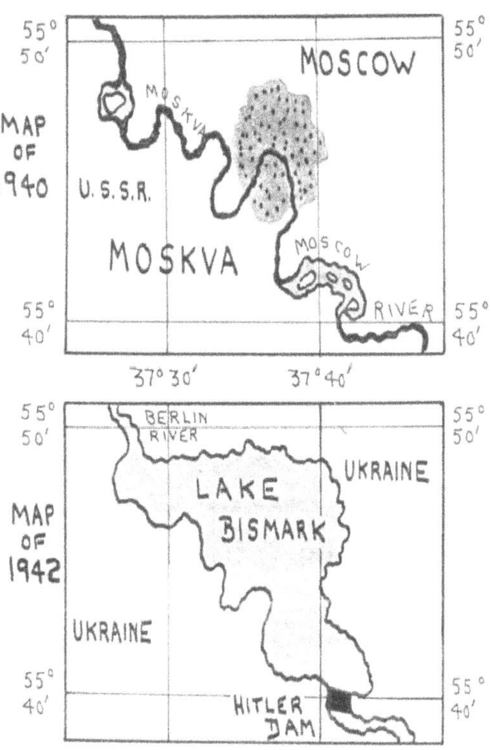

Herr Hitler:
"This is my finest hour"

SYNOPSIS

Pacific Summit

While Hitler's Nazis were consolidating power in Europe, Japan's military was waging aggressive wars on the mainland of Asia.

Vice President Lindbergh, concerned about safety for Americans in Asia, called for a summit with Emperor Hirohito to create a peaceful co-existence!

OFFICE OF VICE PRESIDENT
U.S.A.
Washington, D.C.

M O S T   S E C R E T

January 9, 1942

Chancellor Hitler:

I wish to bring to your attention my concerns about Japans recent aggressive military actions on the mainland of Asia. I am especially concerned about the safety of our American citizens living, working or visiting the far East.

I call upon your services to influence General Hideki Tojo's military government to arrange for a face-to-face talk with Emperor Hirohito so as to preserve peace and friendship between our two nations.

I remain,

Charles A. Lindbergh

Reich Chancellery
Berlin, Deutschland

<u>MOST SECRET</u>

January 12, 1942

President Willkie:

I have given your request careful consideration. I understand your concerns and agree with you that a pacific summit would be desirable.

Since I have a good working relationship with General Tojo, I took the necessary steps to secure a positive response from the Imperial Japanese Emperor. I advise you to extend an invitation to meet Emperor Hirohito somewhere in the pacific realm.

Yours,

Adolf Hitler

OFFICE OF VICE PRESIDENT
U.S.A.
Washington, D.C.

January 9, 1942

Emperor Hirohito:

As leaders of the two most powerful countries a
long the Pacific rim, I suggest we meet to discuss
all matters of mutual interest, such as: security -
culture - investments. If you agree, I am willing to
meet you you in the Pacific region.

I remain,

Charles A. Lindbergh

February, 6 1942

Dear Mr. Lindbergh:
It would be an honor to meet the vice president
of the United States. I agree with your "open"
agenda. Due to historic custom, an Emperor
cannot leave his homeland. A two day summit on
the island of Okinawa: March 9-10 is acceptable.

Emperor Hirohito

MANILA HEMP

Hot   Manila, Philippines   March 11, 1942

PHILIPPINES GRANTED INDEPENDENCE!

At the Pacific summit of Okinawa, vice president Lindbergh told Emperor Hirohito that he would ask Congress to approve independence on January 1, 1943. Hirohito assured Lindbergh that Japan would respect Philippines sovereignty provided she remained neutral!

Other agreed items were:

1. Respect each other's sovereignty

2. Non-interference in domestic and foreign affairs

3. Safety assured for Americans living or visiting Asia

4. U.S. military forces will stay east of Wake Island

5. Japan to respect rights of neutrals

6. Expand trade and cultural exchanges.

| Rain | Peking, China | September 9, 1942 |

THE FALL OF CHINA NEAR

China's long war with Japan is almost over! Japanese forces have been capturing many large cities and centers of communications. Japanese naval forces have a complete blockade of all east coast seaports. President Chaing K'ai-shek has retreated his national government to the interior of China.

Japan has offered to create a united council of China with the intent to transform China into a Japanese protectorate!

Sun   Tokyo, Japan   January 20, 1943

10 YEARS OF SINO-JAPANESE HOSTILITIES END IN VICTORY! CHINA: JAPANESE PROTECTORATE "NEW ORDER" - DECLARED...

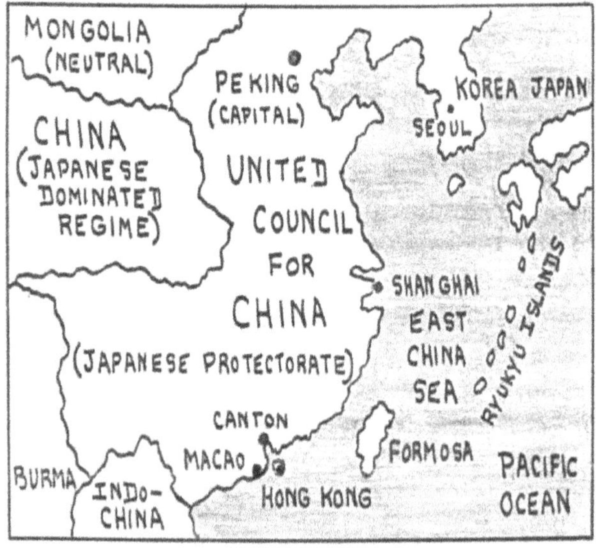

JAPAN'S CONQUEST OF CHINA
KOREA - BURMA - INDO-CHINA
IN THE PACIFIC WAR

Cold	Tokyo, Japan	February 7, 1943

SOVIET-SIBERIA MILITARY SURRENDER TO THE POWERFUL ARMY AND NAVY OF IMPERIAL JAPAN

After a 6 month blockade and siege of the Soviet naval base at Vladivostok, Admiral Vladimir Chuikoff requested an armistice. The Imperial War Ministry agreed only if the Soviet army surrenders as well. Fleet Admiral Chuikoff cabled Tokyo that all forces would give up, if they would be allowed to return to the Free Slavic Land near the Urals.

Japan agreed, provided they all disarmed.

The armistice was set for 0900 6 February 1943!

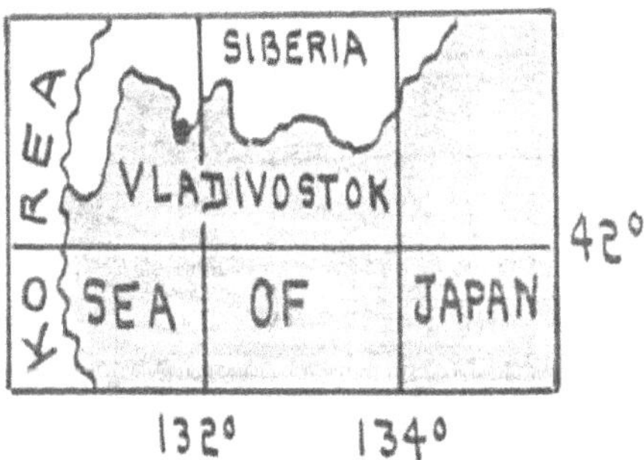

TOKYO RISING SUN

ENGLISH EDITION

Cold	Tokyo, Japan	February 7, 1943

JAPAN - SUPER POWER OF ASIA

FAR EAST ASIA - 1943

AXIS POWER — JAPAN

NEUTRAL NATIONS:

AUSTRALIA • NEW ZEALAND • THAILAND
INDIA • MONGOLIA • PHILIPPINES

SYNOPSIS

Jewish Exodus

One of vice president Charles Lindbergh's highest priorities was his concern for the welfare of all European Jews. He urged the Germans at the Stockholm conference to accept the 1917 Balfour Declaration. Again, at the Azores summit with Hitler, Lindbergh insisted the matter become part of the Atlantic Charter. Since Hitler admired Lindbergh, he agreed to a humane solution to his dilemma.

Budapest Twins

ENGLISH EDITION

Sunny	Budapest, Hungary	May 7, 1943

EXODUS TREATY FOR EUROPEAN JEWS

Diplomats from European Axis powers, neutral nations, World Jewish Congress and the International Red Cross and Crescent, met in Budapest to draw up an exodus plan for Jews of Europe.

TERMS OF AGREEMENT:

1. Jews will have three options:
   a. Live in designated safe and secured European enclaves, b. emigrate to a neutral country, or
   c. live in the Jewish Homeland section of Turkish Palestine
2. Neutral nations to provide funds and ships to evacuate Jews from Europe
3. Axis powers to transport Jews to four embarkation seaports
4. Turkey will administer civil authority for both Palestine Arabs and Jewish Homelands according to the provisions of the Balfour Declaration of 1917
5. Red Cross and Crescent to monitor all living conditions
6. Jewish citizenship granted by Turkey after 3 year residency in Homeland

| Warm | Geneva, Switzerland | May 8, 1943 |

HISTORIC AGREEMENT
IN BUDAPEST

European Jews will have three options for a new life:

1. Safe-secured enclaves

2. Right to emigrate

3. Exodus to Homeland

Axis powers to transport exodus Jews
from four embarkation ports:

Rotterdam — Trieste
Marseilles — Istanbul

EDITORIAL

WJC wish to acknowledge the significant role vice
president Charles A. Lindbergh had in our case:
Stockholm Treaty
Atlantic Charter

Pan American Union

Washington, D.C.   June 5, 1943

LINDBERGH APPEALS TO NEUTRAL NATIONS TO $UPPORT EUROPEAN JEWS

At the 10th Annual Pan American Conference meeting in Lima, Peru, vice president Lindbergh called on all neutral nations to pledge financial aid to millions of Jews trying to secure a safe new life. He urged all 21 Pan-American countries to set up an international Jewish assistance fund to be administered by the Pan-American Union in Washington, D.C. Funds will be allocated by the European Red Cross in Geneva, Switzerland.

FINANCIAL AID WILL COMPENSATE JEWS FOR THE LOSS OF ASSETS AND PROPERTY

OFFICE OF VICE PRESIDENT
U.S.A.
Washington, D.C.

June 7, 1943

Mr. Neville Chamberlain:

At the recent Pan-American Conference, I
called on all 21 neutral nations to pledge
financial aid to European Jews as a form
of compensation for their loss of assets and
property as a result of the recent war.
Positive response resulted! As Prime
Minister of Great Britain, I urge you to
appeal to all neutrals of Europe to join the
American states in this noble cause!

I remain,

Charles A. Lindbergh

ISTANBUL CONFERENCE ON HOMELANDS FOR JEWS AND ARABS IN PALESTINE

As directed by the Budapest accords, Turkey is to administer civil authority in Palestine. The ten day Istanbul Conference attended by diplomats from the Arab League, World Jewish Congress and the Turkish Foreign Office, developed specific boundaries for Jewish and Arab towns. It was also agreed that Jerusalem is to be an "open city" to all faiths, but administered by a tripartite council consisting of 3 Jews, 3 Arabs and 3 Turks from the Ankara government. Civil administration of both homelands is granted to the Tripartite Council. All Council actions will be subject to review by the Turkish government.

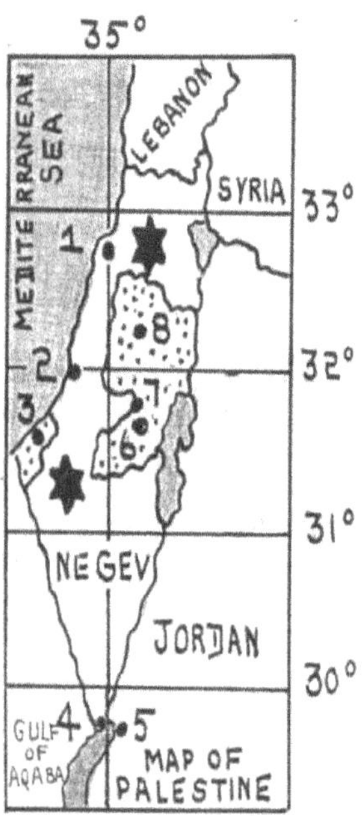

KEY TO MAP

 ARABS

 JEWS

1. Haifa 2. Tel Aviv 3. Gaza
4. Elat 5. Aqaba 6. Bethlehem
7. Jerusalem 8. Nabulus

𝔖𝔱𝔬𝔠𝔨𝔥𝔬𝔩𝔪 𝔇𝔬𝔳𝔢

English Edition

| Fair | Stockholm, Sweden | May 5, 1944 |

Nobel Prize Committee:

NOBEL PEACE PRIZE

1944

AWARDED TO

CHARLES A. LINDBERGH

VICE PRESIDENT OF THE U.S.A.

<u>ACHIEVEMENTS:</u>

EXODUS PLAN FOR JEWS

TREATY OF STOCKHOLM - '40

ATLANTIC CHARTER - '41

JEWISH RELIEF FUND - '43

SYNOPSIS

World Government

With the Axis powers in control of the Eastern hemisphere and the Neutral Nations in control of the Western hemisphere, there was a call on both sides to build a bridge of trust connecting them. The Axis leaders agreed, and created a World Government in Dresden, Germany, to be known as the Organization of Supreme States!

O.S.S.

Istanbul ☪ Crescent

| Rain | Istanbul, Turkey | June 14, 1943 |

TURKEY - AXIS POWER IN NEAR EAST!

NEAR EAST - 1943

AXIS POWERS
ITALY • BULGARIA
TURKEY • UKRAINE

NEUTRAL NATIONS
SAUDI ARABIA • IRAN
AFGHANISTAN

PALESTINE
(1)HOMELAND FOR JEWS
(2)HOMELAND FOR ARABS

ROME FASCIST

ENGLISH EDITION

| Sunny | Rome, Italy | June 10, 1943 |

TREATY OF ROME DIVIDES AFRICA

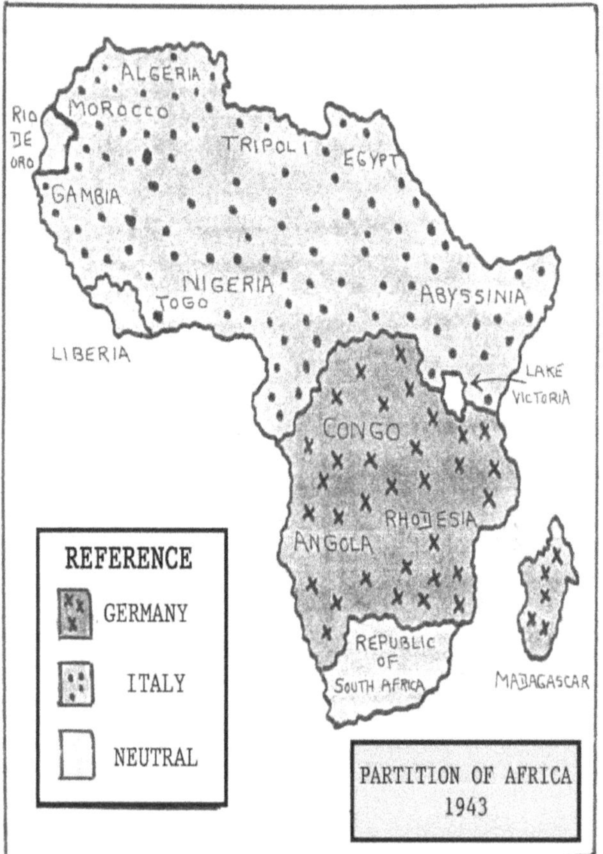

GREAT DAY FOR OUR DUCE!

Hot	Cairo, Egypt (Italy)	June 20, 1943

EGYPTIANS APPOINTED TO THE AXIS CONTROL SUEZ CANAL AUTHORITY BOARD

Antonio Giresi, High Commissioner for the Italian Province of Egypt, announced - the newly created ASCA Board will be composed of 5 members, 3 appointed by Rome and 2 by our Cairo government. The Board will administer daily operations of the Suez Canal. All revenues will be divided · 60% Goes to Rome, and 40% for Cairo.

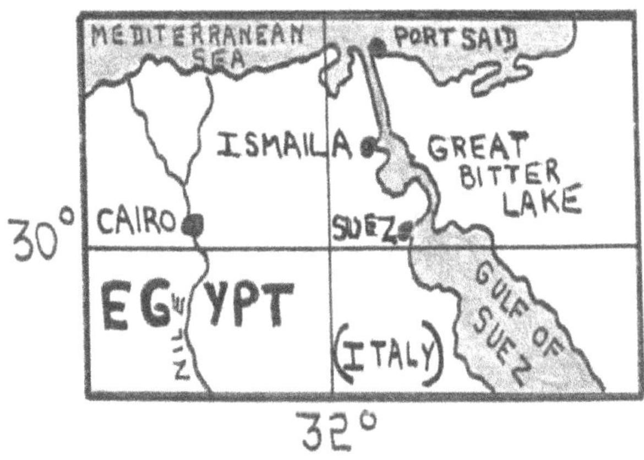

SUPREME STATES
CHARTER

Six weeks ago - Der Führer invited leaders from Axis powers and Neutral nations to Dresden to create a global organization! Today all 50 nations signed the Dresden Treaty creating - **O.S.S.** Organization of Supreme States.

SUPREME STATES CHARTER:

1. Assembly of States
2. Security Council - 6 permanent members: Germania, Italy, Japan, Finland, Ukraine and Turkey - and 7 non-permanent members elected by the Assembly for a 3 year term.
3. Procedures, functions and powers are outlined in articles 3-21.

DRESDEN PULSE

ENGLISH EDITION

WARM   -   DRESDEN, GERMANY   -   JUNE 6, 1944

SUPREME STATES
WORLD HEADQUARTERS
DEDICATED

HERR HITLER WILL CUT RIBBON TO OPEN SS FACILITIES TO DELEGATES FROM 50 NATIONS AND WORLD-WIDE VISITORS

Boston Patriots

5¢

HUMAN RIGHTS
FOR OCCUPIED PEOPLE
ENDORSED BY S.S.

The Assembly of States of the Supreme States in Dresden, Germania, adopted the American resolution calling upon the Security Council of the S.S. to establish a Human Rights Commission. HRCOP Commission would be charged with drafting a charter of human rights which is to be submitted to the Assembly of States for Final Action by October 1. Assembly approved the American resolution: 39 to 11!

DRESDEN PULSE

ENGLISH EDITION

HOT   -   DRESDEN, GERMANY   -   JUNE 21, 1944

PERMANENT WINTER-SUMMER OLYMPIC VILLAGES FOR 1948 APPROVED BY S.S. ASSMEBLY OF STATES 32 TO 18!

SYNOPSIS

Germania

Adolf Hitler, Europe's new Napoleon, envisioned an expanded Germany to be called - Germania!

This new center of European power would become a melting pot of Aryans and defeated Nationals: French, Belgians, Dutch, Danes and Poles. Hitler never liked the Berlin Prussians, so he decided to build a new capital city in Nürnberg. To show his love for art, Hitler ordered the building of an art center reflecting world art. He asked President Willkie to select art for the American wing.

AXIS POWERS:

GERMANIA • ITALY • TURKEY
HUNGARY • RUMANIA • BULGARIA • UKRAINE

NUETRAL NATIONS:

UNITED KINGDOM • IRELAND • SWEDEN
SPAIN • PORTUGAL • SWITZERLAND

GERMAN-DOMINATED REGIMES:

VICHY • NORWAY

July 4, 1944

President Willkie:

As you know Germania's new capital is now Nürnberg.
To celebrate the opening of our National Arts Center on
August 15, 1944, I would consider it an honor if you would
select 20 or 30 portraits of Americans at work or play to be
displayed in the American wing of our art gallery.

Yours,

Adolf Hitler

THE WHITE HOUSE
WASHINGTON, D.C.

July 9, 1944

Chancellor Hitler:

Thank you for your kind invitation. I have
consulted with our National Arts Commission,
and they have selected a young talented
artist who has a wonderful collection called:
Good Life. Your Arts Commission should
receive, within two weeks, 20 - 30 pieces of
his art showing slices of Americana.
Exhibit should please you.

I remain,

Wendell Willkie

GERMANIA ART GALLERY

AMERICAN WING PRESENTS
September 7—November 5, 1944

GOOD LIFE
PORTRAIT EXHIBIT
AMERICAN ARTIST
COURTNEY CHRISTOPHER AMERSON

New Orleans Jazz	G.Q. Men
Singers Unlimited	Shades
New York Dancin'	Mid-West Hair Style
Good Friends	Sculptures
Classy Ladies	Mardi Gras Royalty

jazzY

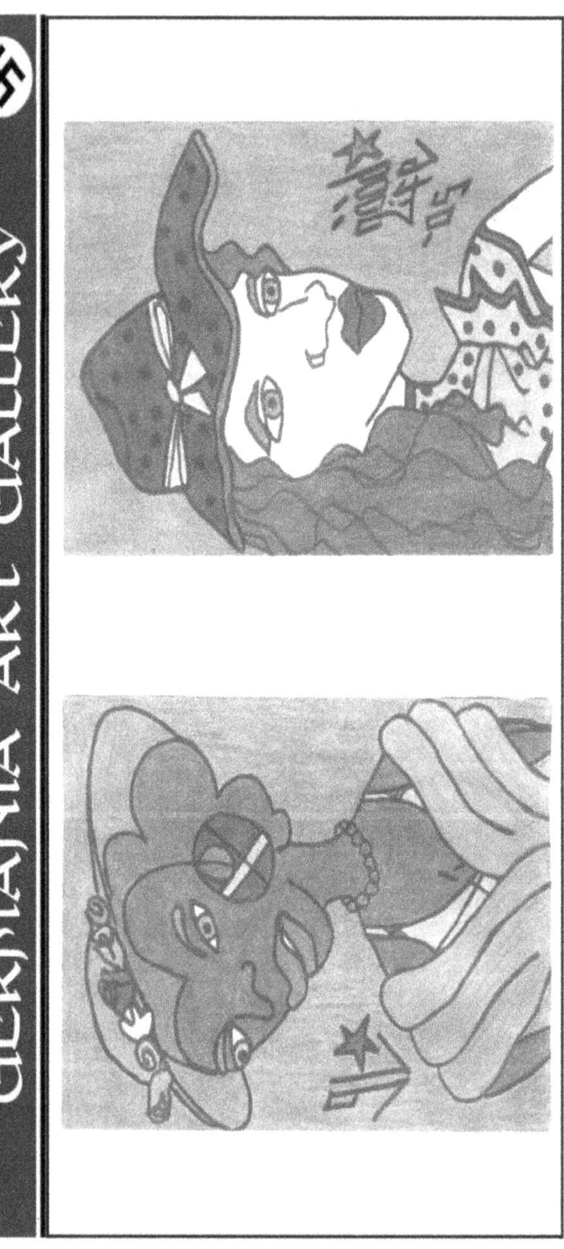

GOOD
life

SYNOPSIS

Back to Reality

On the morning of August 8, 1936, Adolf Hitler's long night of "twisted fantasy" came to an abrupt end when he was awakened by his valet. After a hardy German breakfast, he proceeded to the Olympic stadium with anticipation of viewing his Aryans winning more gold! However, one athlete destroyed his desire to see more Nordic victory, that athlete was - Jesse Owens!

PITTSBURG HARDHATS

5¢

Hot	Pittsburg, Pennsylvania	August 9, 1936

JESSE OWENS WINS GOLD!

A TRUE AFRICAN-AMERICAN HERO

JESSE WINS FOUR GOLD MEDALS AT THE BERLIN OLYMPICS

OWENS STUNNING VICTORIES - WON IN NAZI GERMANY - IS A SALUTE TO BLACK PRIDE AND A BLOW TO SUPERIORITY OF ARYAN PEOPLE!

100 Meter Dash
10.3 seconds

200 Meter Dash
20.7 seconds

Broad Jump
26', 5¼"

4x100 Meter
Relay: 39.8 seconds
Owens
Metcalf
Draper
Wykoff

INTERNATIONAL OLYMPIC COMMITTEE

1936 BERLIN OLYMPIC RESULTS		
RANK	GOLD	TOTAL
1 DEUTSCHLAND	33	89
2 U.S.A.	24	56
3 HUNGARY	3	16

CITIUS, ALTIUS, FORTIUS

Olympic Motto
Faster, Higher, Stronger

GOOD-BYE BERLIN - 1936!

and...

HELLO TOKYO - 1940!

EPILOGUE

While evil may have given Nazi Germany, in the short run, victory of winning the most gold and total medals the Berlin Olympics - in the long run - good triumphed by the Jesse Owens accomplishments. Owens blew Adolf Hitler's superiority of the Nordic-Aryan race myth out of the water!

Many years later the good citizens of post-Nazi Germany recognized the Owens Spirit by naming a Berlin street and school in his honor. The long, over due, hand shakes were given at a Berlin Olympic Reunion